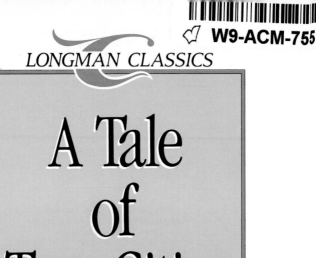

## LONGMAN CLASSICS

# A Tale
# of
# Two Cities

## Charles Dickens

Simplified by D K Swan
Illustrated by Barry Wilkinson

Longman

**Longman Group UK Limited,**
Longman House, Burnt Mill, Harlow,
Essex CM20 2JE, England
and Associated Companies throughout the world.

This simplified edition © Longman Group UK Limited 1991

First published 1991
Fourth impression 1994

# ISBN 0-582-03047-1

Set in 12/14 point Linotron 202 Versailles
Printed in Hong Kong
GC/04

### Acknowledgements

The cover background is a wallpaper design called NUAGE,
courtesy of Osborne and Little plc.

### Stage 2 : 900 word vocabulary

Please look under *New words* at the back of this book
for explanations of words outside this stage.

# Contents

# Introduction

*Charles Dickens*
Charles Dickens was born in 1812. He was the son of a clerk in a government office. His father was perhaps rather like Mr Micawber in Dickens's *David Copperfield* (1849), spending more money than he earned. At that time a man could be sent to prison if he owed money and could not pay it, and that is what happened to Charles Dickens's father. The result was very bad for Charles himself. He was twelve years old when his father went to prison, and Charles had to leave school and go to work – very unpleasant work, with bad pay and conditions.

Charles visited his father in prison, and he never forgot the experience. In *A Tale of Two Cities* Dickens describes the state of Dr Manette when he first comes out of the Bastille prison. That must have been the condition of many of the people Dickens saw in prison in London.

By the time *A Tale of Two Cities* appeared in 1859, Charles Dickens was already well known as a writer. His first great success was *The Pickwick Papers* (1836). That was followed by a number of novels: *Oliver Twist* (1838), *Nicholas Nickleby* (1839), *The Old Curiosity Shop* (1840),

*Barnaby Rudge* (1841), *A Christmas Carol* (1843), *Dombey and Son* (1846), *David Copperfield* (1849), *Bleak House* (1853) and *Hard Times* (1854).

The stories are full of characters – some of them invented, many of them people that Dickens had seen and studied. Some of them we love, like Mr Lorry, who calls himself "just a business machine", but who has a surprisingly kind heart. Some we hate, like the really hard-hearted marquis, or the lying John Barsad.

Charles Dickens knew his "two cities" – knew London well, and knew Paris from a number of visits between 1844 and 1858. Before writing, and often while writing the book, he made close study of Carlyle's *The French Revolution*, and in 1845 he had talked to Jules Michelet, the French historian of the Revolution. He also met other French writers, and old people who remembered the Revolution.

*The French Revolution*
There were a number of causes of the French Revolution, which began in 1789. The cause that is important in this book is the misuse of power by the noble families, the aristocrats, who treated the common people so badly. Examples of this misuse of power are the hanging of Gaspard, the cruel death of a woman and her brother who displeased the Marquis St Evrémonde, and the use of a *lettre de cachet* (page 7)

to send Dr Manette to prison in the Bastille.

These things led to violence like the attack on the Bastille on 14 July 1789 and the death at the guillotine of aristocrats and their supporters – and later of those who displeased the party in power.

Dickens took his description of the storming of the Bastille, and the scene at the guillotine from Carlyle's *The French Revolution* (1837). That long history contains many details such as the row of knitting women sitting in front of the crowd at the guillotine, counting the cut-off heads, like fans counting the score at a sporting match today.

There is a lesson in *A Tale of Two Cities*. Dickens makes it clear that a class that does evil – as the French aristocrats did – will in the end suffer evil. But he does not call for violent change – he is not a revolutionary. We are to believe that if all the French nobles had willingly tried to help the people, as Darnay did; if French thinkers had shown up the evil, as Dr Manette tried to do; if all men were ready to give their lives for their friends, as Sydney Carton did; if there were more kindness like Mr Lorry's, then the world would be better, and there would be no revolutions and no dangerous crowds of angry citizens.

# Chapter 1
## From London to Dover

The first person in our story travelled on the coach from London to Dover in November 1775. The coach stopped at the top of Shooter's Hill to let the four horses breathe after the long climb. It was a dark night with a thick mist.

"Listen!" the coach driver called to the guard.

"Yes," the guard answered. "A horse coming up behind us – fast!" And he held the first of his guns ready. When the sound was quite near, he called out, as loudly as he could: "Ho, there! Stop! Or I'll shoot!"

They heard the rider stop his horse, and a man's voice called from the mist, "Is that the Dover coach?"

"Why do you want to know?" answered the guard.

"I have to speak to a passenger, if it is."

"What passenger?"

"Mr Jarvis Lorry."

"Stay where you are," the guard called to the voice in the mist, "because if I make a mistake, you won't be alive to tell me. Gentleman of the name of Lorry, answer."

Mr Lorry got down into the road.

"Who wants me? Is it Jerry Cruncher?"

"Yes, Mr Lorry. A message from Tellson's."

"I know this messenger, guard," said Mr Lorry. "You can let him come close. I work for Tellson's Bank."

"Come very slowly," the guard called to the horseman.

Mr Lorry opened the message and read it by the light of the lamp on his side of the coach:

"WAIT AT DOVER FOR MISS MANETTE."

"Jerry," said Mr Lorry, "tell them that I got the message and I'll wait."

The coach reached Dover in the morning, and the head waiter of the Royal George Hotel opened the door for Mr Lorry to get out. The other passengers had all left the coach at earlier stopping places.

"There will be a boat for Calais tomorrow, will there, waiter?" asked Mr Lorry.

"Yes, sir, if the wind is right and the sea not too rough. The tide will be right at about two in the afternoon. A bedroom, sir?"

"Yes, please. But I won't go to bed until tonight. I'll just wash and change. Then I'll have breakfast, please."

When Mr Lorry came down to breakfast, the people of the hotel saw a well-dressed business man about sixty years old. He wore a good brown suit, and while he waited for his breakfast, he sat very still. Only his eyes moved, seeing everything in the room without seeming

*Mr Lorry reaches Dover*

to look at anything. They were bright eyes, and their owner must have had some trouble in the past, training them to the serious look expected of one who worked for Tellson's Bank.

When his breakfast arrived, he said to the head waiter, "Please ask them to prepare a room for a young lady who may come here at any time today. She may ask for Mr Jarvis Lorry, or she may only ask for a gentleman from Tellson's Bank. Please tell me at once when she arrives."

"Yes, sir. Tellson's Bank in London, sir? We are often visited by your gentlemen travelling between London and Paris, sir. Your gentlemen travel a lot. But I don't think we have seen you, yourself, sir."

"No. It's fifteen years since we ... since I last came from France."

It was after Mr Lorry's dinner that he heard wheels coming along the narrow street and turning into the hotel yard. "Here she is!" he said to himself.

In a few minutes, the waiter came and told him that Miss Manette had arrived from London, and she would like to see the gentleman from Tellson's as soon as possible.

The gentleman from Tellson's stood up. He did not seem very happy as he followed the waiter to Miss Manette's rooms. There he found a young lady not more than seventeen years old. She was pretty. Mr Lorry noticed that her forehead – young and unlined – had gathered itself in a way that showed – not uncertainty, not wonder, not fear, but something of all these, and mostly a bright attention. It made him suddenly remember a small child he had held in his arms on a crossing from Calais to Dover many years before.

"Please sit down," she said. "I received a letter from the bank yesterday, sir. It told me that there was some information – some news – about something belonging to my father. – My poor father! I never saw him! So long dead! – This news, it seems, made it necessary for me to go to Paris, and there I had to meet a gentleman from the bank, who was being sent to Paris to help me. I answered that I was ready to go, but I said I would like to travel with the gentleman from the bank, because I would be alone. The gentleman had left London, but the bank sent a messenger after him, asking him to wait for me here."

"I was glad to receive the message," said Mr Lorry, "and it will please me to serve you."

"Thank you. Thank you very much. The bank said that the gentleman would tell me about the business. They said I must prepare myself for a surprise. Naturally I am interested to hear about the matter."

"Naturally," said Mr Lorry. "Yes ... I ... er ... It's very difficult to begin."

The young forehead lifted itself in the way he had already noticed. "Are you quite a stranger to me, sir?" she asked.

"Miss Manette, I am a man of business, and I am here on business. You must hear me as just a speaking machine, nothing else. You must allow me, if you please, to tell you the story of one of the bank's customers."

"Story?"

He seemed to mistake the word she had questioned, as he hurried on, "Yes, customers. In the banking business we usually call the people who use our services our customers. He was a French gentleman, a man of great knowledge – a doctor."

"Not of Beauvais?"

"Well, yes, of Beauvais, like Dr Manette, your father. And like Dr Manette, your father, he was well known in Paris. I knew him there, as one of our customers. I was at that time in our Paris office."

"'At that time' – may I ask at what time, sir?"

"I am speaking, miss, of twenty years ago. He married an English lady, and I dealt with the business side of the marriage. Just business, you understand. Without friendship or feelings. In such matters I am just a business machine."

"But——" The curiously roughened forehead was there again. "But this is my father's story, sir. And I am beginning to think that when my mother died only two years after his death, *you* brought me to England. I am almost sure it was you."

"Yes, Miss Manette. That's true. And the fact that I haven't seen you since then shows that I really am just a man of business without feelings. I have no time for feelings. I spend my whole life turning a huge money machine. – As you say, it is like the sad story of your father. But now we come to the difference. If your father hadn't died— Don't be frightened!"

She had caught his arm with both her hands.

"Please," said Mr Lorry, putting his own hand on the small shaking hands, "please don't let anything I say hurt you. – A matter of business. As I was saying ..."

Her look troubled him so much that he stopped. He thought hard for a minute, and then he began again.

"As I was saying, suppose Dr Manette had not died. You know that in France a person with power can get a paper – a *lettre de cachet*. That *lettre de cachet* can cause an enemy to disappear – to be taken secretly to a prison, and kept there. Suppose Dr Manette had disappeared like that. Suppose his wife had tried to get news about him – from even the king, the queen, the church, the chief men of the government – and suppose she had learnt nothing from any of them. If you suppose all those things, then the story of Dr Manette would be like the story of our customer, the doctor from Beauvais."

The young hands closed more tightly on his arm.

"It *is* my father's story. Why did I never know?"

Mr Lorry took a deep breath. "Be brave!" he said. "Business! Yes, it's true. Your mother suffered such great pain in her uncertainty that she decided that you must not be told. She was still trying to get news – any news – of your father when she died – of a broken heart. You were two years old, and on her death-bed she ordered that you should be allowed to grow up without the dark cloud of uncertainty – uncertainty whether your father soon died in prison or lived on in misery for many years."

He saw in her face the pain that he had tried not to cause her. He said, "They haven't found something belonging to your father. He himself has been – found. He is alive. Perhaps greatly changed – though we must have hope – but alive. Your father has been taken to the house in Paris of a man who was once his servant. And we are going there: I to say, I hope, that he really is Dr Manette; and you to bring him back to life, love, rest, comfort."

## Chapter 2
## In Paris

The wine-shop stood in the poorest part of Paris, in Saint Antoine. Its customers came when they had a little money. But there was very little money in Saint Antoine – very little money, very little food, very little clothing.

The wine-shop keeper, Defarge, was a strong-looking man, dark, with good eyes. He looked kind, but not quick to forgive an enemy – a man not easily turned when he had started in one direction.

Madame Defarge, his wife, was sitting near the door as he came in. She, too, was strong-looking, with watchful eyes. She said nothing when her husband came in, but a very small movement told him to look round the wine-shop. There were not many customers. He knew the five men of Saint Antoine who were making a very little wine last as long as possible. The two strangers were a gentleman in a brown suit – not French – and a young lady.

"What are *they* doing here?" Defarge wondered.

The gentleman in the brown suit came towards him. They spoke a few words, and then Defarge left the wine-shop. Madame Defarge was knitting, and she seemed to see nothing as the gentleman led the young lady out through the door that Defarge had used.

In the dark entrance to some dark stairs, Defarge went down on one knee to kiss the hand of the daughter of the man who was once his employer. It was a gentle action, but he was not now a gentle servant. He had become a secret, angry, dangerous man.

"It is very high," he said, pointing to the stairs. "It is better to begin slowly." They spoke in French. Mr Lorry had spent a number of years in Tellson's in Paris, and he knew the language well.

"Is he alone?" Mr Lorry asked very quietly.

"Alone! Who could be with him?" Defarge said in the same low voice.

"Is he always alone, then?"

"Yes."

"By his own wish?"

"By his own necessity. He is as he was when I first saw him – when they found me and asked if I would take him – and told me that I must say nothing, or I would be in great danger."

"Is he greatly changed?" Mr Lorry asked.

"Changed!" The keeper of the wine-shop struck the wall with his hand. It was the clearest answer.

They climbed higher and higher, to the top of the stairs. Then Defarge took out a key.

"You think it is necessary to keep the door locked?" asked Mr Lorry.

"I think it is necessary to turn the key."

"Why?"

"Because he has lived so long locked up in the Bastille that he would be frightened – driven out of his mind – if he didn't hear the key."

Defarge made as much noise as possible with the key. He unlocked the door and pushed it open. Then he looked into the room and said something. A weak voice answered something that the visitors could not hear.

The wine-shop keeper showed them by a sign that they should enter the little room.

Mr Lorry put his arm round the daughter, afraid that she would faint. "Er . . . er . . . business! Business!" he said.

With his back towards the door, and his face towards the small window, a white-haired man sat on a low wooden seat. He was bent forward and very busy, making shoes.

"Good morning," said Defarge.

A very weak voice answered after a moment: "Good morning."

"You have a visitor, as you see."

The shoemaker did not stop working.

"Listen," said Defarge."Here is your visitor, who knows a well-made shoe when he sees one. Show him that shoe. Take it, sir."

Mr Lorry took it in his hand.

"Tell the visitor what kind of shoe it is, and the name of the maker."

There was silence for nearly a minute before the shoemaker answered: "I forget what you asked me. What did you say?"

"I said, 'Please describe the kind of shoe.'"

"It is a lady's shoe. It is the newest kind."

"And the maker's name?" said Defarge.

Another long silence. Then: "Did you ask me for my name?"

"Yes."

"One hundred and five, North Tower."

"Is that all?"

"One hundred and five, North Tower."

"You were not always a shoemaker?" said Mr Lorry.

Another long silence. "I was not always a shoemaker? No, I was not. I learnt it here. I taught myself. I asked permission to teach myself." Silence. "I got permission with great difficulty after a long time, and I have made shoes ever since."

He held out his hand for the shoe that Mr Lorry was holding.

Mr Lorry gave him the shoe, then looked closely at his face. "Doctor Manette," he said, "don't you remember me? Don't you remember this man?" He put his hand on Defarge's arm. "Look at him. Look at me. Don't you remember a banker from long ago – business from long ago – a servant from long ago?"

It seemed that, for a moment, the black mist that had fallen on the shoemaker's mind partly cleared. Marks of active thought appeared on his forehead. They disappeared. But they were there long enough for Mr Lorry to see that it really was his old friend – or "customer".

Mr Lorry looked from the shoemaker to the lovely young woman, and he saw on her forehead the same marks of thought and anxiety. She had moved very near to her father, and after a time he looked up.

"Who are you?"

Not yet sure that she could control her voice, she sat down on the seat beside him. He moved away a little in surprise, but she put her hand on his arm.

He turned quickly – so quickly that Mr Lorry and Defarge were afraid. But she stopped them with a sign. Slowly and lovingly she took the poor, white-headed man in her arms.

They sat like that for a long time, saying nothing.

At last Mr Lorry and Defarge stepped forward to take some action.

She held up her hand. "Can you arrange for us to leave Paris at once?" she said, in French so that Defarge would understand.

"But is he able to make the journey?" asked Mr Lorry.

"Better able to do that, I think, than to stay in this city where he has suffered so much."

"It is true," said Defarge. "More than that: for all reasons, Dr Manette is best out of

*Lucie puts her hand on her father's arm*

France.   Shall I get a carriage and horses?"

"That's business," said Mr Lorry, suddenly remembering to be a business machine.   "And if business is to be done, I must do it."

There were other things to be done besides getting a carriage and horses, so Mr Lorry and Defarge both left the little room.   "Don't be anxious about me," she had said.

It was dark when they came back with travelling papers, thick coats, bread and meat, wine, and hot coffee.   Like a man who has been forced to obey for many years, Dr Manette ate and drank what they gave him.   He put on the coat and hat that they gave him to wear.   He willingly went with his daughter when she put her arm through his, and he took – and kept – her hand in both his own hands.

When they reached the street, there were no people to be seen except Madame Defarge – who was knitting at the wine-shop door, and saw nothing.

He had climbed into the carriage, and his daughter had followed him, when he asked miserably for his shoemaking things and the un-finished shoes.   Madame Defarge immediately called to her husband that she would get them. She quickly brought them down and passed them in – and immediately afterwards went back to knitting at the wine-shop door, and saw nothing.

# Chapter 3
## The trial

Tellson's London office was quite near the Law Courts. Outside Tellson's – never in it unless he was called in – was an odd-job-man and messenger, Jerry Cruncher.

Five years after Dr Manette came back to London, on a day in the year 1780, one of Tellson's oldest workers called for Jerry Cruncher.

"Go to the Law Courts," he said. "Find the door where the witnesses go in, and show this note to the doorkeeper. He will let you in and will give the note to Mr Lorry."

"Must I wait in the court, sir?" Jerry asked.

"Yes. Until Mr Lorry wants you."

Inside the court, Jerry asked the man next to him, "What's on?"

"A spy."

"Hanging?" asked Jerry.

"No," said the man. "Quartering." And he added, with great pleasure: "They'll cut his head off and cut his body into quarters. That's what they'll do."

"If he's guilty," Jerry added.

"Oh, they'll say he's guilty! You can be sure of that."

Jerry looked round the court.

Mr Lorry was sitting among the lawyers, quite near to the prisoner's lawyer, who had a large number of papers in front of him. Almost facing him, there was another lawyer, who had his hands in his pockets, and seemed to be interested only in the ceiling.

After a time, two officers brought in the prisoner. He was a young gentleman, about twenty-five years old, good-looking and strong.

"Silence in court!"

"Charles Darnay," the lawyer for the Crown said, "is on trial because he has helped the enemies of our most excellent, splendid, and famous king, having, at different times and in different ways, given information to help Lewis, the French king, in his wars against our most excellent, splendid, and famous king. He has done this by coming and going between the country of our most excellent, splendid, and famous king and the country of the said French Lewis. In doing this, he has given to the said French Lewis lists of the forces that our most excellent, splendid, and famous king was sending to Canada and North America." And so on and so forth – endlessly, Jerry Cruncher thought.

It was all too difficult for Jerry, and his eyes began to wander round the court. It was then that he saw two people who did not seem to belong to the world of courts and trials. One was a young lady, not much more than twenty years old. The other was clearly her father. He was noticeable because of the whiteness of his hair and the thoughtful look of his face – the look of one whose thoughts are turned in. With that look on his face, he seemed old. But when it changed – as now, in speaking to his daughter – he became a good-looking man, not old at all. The young lady sat close to him and held his hand. She was clearly anxious that the trial should not hurt him in any way. But it was also clear that she was deeply touched by pity for the prisoner.

"Who are they?" Jerry asked.

The man next to him did not know, but at last the answer came back: "Witnesses."

"For which side?"

Again the question seemed to go a long way before the answer came: "Against the prisoner."

The chief witness for the Crown – and against the prisoner, Charles Darnay – was John Barsad. The lawyer for the Crown showed that Barsad was an excellent man who, for love of his country, had told the servants of the Crown about Darnay and the lists he had given to Frenchmen.

Mr Stryver, Darnay's lawyer, had some very good questions to ask Barsad.

"Have you ever been a spy yourself?"

"No. How dare anybody say so?"

"What do you live on?"

"My land."

"Where is your land?"

"I don't remember exactly."

"Have you ever been in prison?"

"Certainly not."

"Never in prison for stealing?"

"Why should that question be asked?"

"Never in prison for stealing? Answer again. Never?"

"Yes."

"How many times?"

"Two or three times."

"Not five or six?"

"Perhaps."

And so it continued until it was quite clear that John Barsad was a spy himself, paid to give information against others.

Then it was Mr Lorry's turn. The Crown wanted him to say that Charles Darnay was a passenger on the night coach when Mr Lorry travelled to Dover.

"I can't say that," said Mr Lorry.

"But," said the Crown, "can you truthfully say that he was not one of them?"

"We were all wearing so much that it was impossible to see anyone's face or shape."

"So the prisoner *could* have been one of them?"

"Yes. – Except that he doesn't seem to be a man who would easily be frightened. All the passengers on that coach were very frightened by the thought of gun-carrying highwaymen."

Miss Manette was called. The Crown

wanted to show that Charles Darnay was on the boat when she and Mr Lorry brought her father back to England. Two French gentlemen were with him when he came on board. She did not hear what they said, and she did not know anything about any papers they might have had.

Next, the Crown called a witness to show that Darnay had been seen in a hotel in a town where ships were made ready to carry army forces overseas. The witness had never seen Darnay before or since, but he was quite sure the prisoner was the man he had seen in the town. Stryver was not being so successful in breaking down this witness. But just then the lawyer who had been interested only in the ceiling moved. He wrote a few words on a piece of paper and passed it to Stryver.

Stryver looked at the note. "You are quite sure," he said to the witness, "that it was the prisoner?"

The witness was quite sure.

Stryver said, "Did you ever see anybody very like the prisoner?"

"Not so like the prisoner that I could have made a mistake."

"Will you please look at my friend here," Stryver said to the judge, "and then look at the prisoner. Would a mistake be impossible?"

The friend was less carefully dressed and less healthy-looking than the prisoner, but they were so much like each other that the judge, the witness, and all the other people in court were surprised. After that, it was quite easy for Stryver to break this witness and show that his story was worthless.

Mr Carton, the lawyer who was so much like the prisoner, went back to looking at the ceiling. But he saw more than he seemed to see. When Miss Manette's head dropped on her father's shoulder, he was the first to see it, and to say to the doorkeeper: "Officer! Help the gentleman to take that young lady out. Can't you see that she needs fresh air?"

It was not long before Mr Lorry gave Jerry a piece of paper on which he had written: NOT GUILTY. "Take that to the bank quickly, Jerry," he said. "It is a very good result for this trial, which ought never to have started."

Sydney Carton, who seemed to be the laziest and most careless of men, was Stryver's great helper. Other lawyers had thought, at one time, that Stryver was not very good at his work. Although he was a good speaker, and clever with words, he was not good at seeing the important points in a large number of papers, as a lawyer must. But then he began to work with Sydney Carton, and after that, Stryver always had the important points ready and well arranged when he went into court. Sydney Carton could work hard and carefully when he wanted to.

After the trial of Charles Darnay, the door of Stryver's office was opened by Stryver himself at about ten o'clock, and Sydney Carton went in.

"That was a good point that you made, Sydney, about your looking like Darnay," said Stryver. "How did you notice it?"

"I thought he was rather a good-looking fellow. And I thought I would have been the same kind of fellow if I'd had any luck."

"You and your luck, Sydney!" laughed Stryver. "You're always talking about your bad luck! Well, let's get to work. Only two trials to prepare for tonight."

"Give me the more difficult first."

Stryver gave his friend a great load of papers, then lay back in an easy chair. Sydney Carton started work, preparing Stryver's court work for the next day. His mind was so busy that his eyes did not even follow the hand that reached out – more and more often – for his glass. They worked – or Sydney Carton worked – until three o'clock in the morning.

"And now," said Stryver, "we've finished. One more drink. You were very good today. Every question I asked those Crown witnesses was a good one."

"My questions are always good, aren't they?" He sounded hurt – almost angry.

"The old Sydney Carton of Shrewsbury School," said Stryver. "Up one minute and down the next."

"Ah!" said his friend. "Yes. The same Sydney, with the same luck. Even at school I did exercises for the other boys instead of doing my own. Even when you and I were students together in Paris, learning the French language and French law, you were always somewhere, and I was always – nowhere."

"And why was that?"

"I don't know. Perhaps it was because you were always pushing your way up, so that, with my bad luck, I couldn't do anything except follow."

# Chapter 4
## The marquis

The carriage carrying the marquis travelled at a wild speed through the narrow Paris streets, round corners and between houses.

The marquis was returning from the town house of one of the great lords in power in France. The marquis had hoped for some favour from the lord, but he had not been able to speak to him. The marquis was very angry.

As the carriage rushed round a corner near a wine-shop in Saint Antoine, a wheel hit something, and there was a loud cry from a number of voices. The horses were frightened, and twenty hands reached up to hold them.

"What's the matter?" said the marquis carelessly, looking out.

A tall man in a cap had picked something up from the road and was down on his knees by the side of the street, crying loudly over it.

"Why is he making that noise?" asked the marquis.

An answer came: "Pardon, Monsieur the Marquis. It is his child."

"Why can't you people take care of yourselves and your children? You might have hurt my horses. Give him that." He threw out a gold coin.

The tall man cried out again: "Dead!"

Another man came towards him, and the poor father turned miserably to him.

"I know all about it," the latest arrival said. "Be a brave man, Gaspard! It is better for the poor little thing to die like that – in a moment, without pain – than to live on in these bad times."

"You are a wise man," said the marquis. "What's your name?"

"They call me Defarge."

"This is for you," said the marquis, throwing out another gold coin. And he called out the order: "Drive on."

He sat back in his seat, and the carriage started. But just then a coin was thrown into his carriage. The marquis looked to the place where Defarge had been. He was not there, but in his place was a strong-looking woman, knitting.

Two days later, the marquis's heavy travelling carriage, with its four horses, stopped in the village nearest to his château, his great country house. Everything and everybody in the village was poor. It was quite clear what made them poor. Notices about taxes were on the walls in the little square: the tax for the state, the tax for the church, the tax for the lord, the salt tax, the tax for this and the tax for that. There was a tax for everything.

*The marquis's carriage speeds through the streets of Paris*

The marquis spoke from his carriage to Gabelle, the man who was paid to gather the taxes from the village and the country round it.

After a few minutes, an old road-mender came into the square.

"Bring that fellow here," the marquis ordered Gabelle. Then, when the man was standing in front of him, with his blue cap in his hand, the marquis said, "I passed you on the road?"

"My lord, it is true.  I had the honour to be passed."

"What were you staring at under my carriage?"

"My lord, I was looking at the man."

"The man!" said the Marquis angrily. "What man?  What do you mean?"

"He was hanging under your carriage, my lord.  All covered with dust, he was.  With his head hanging over – like this! He was a tall man, my lord, a stranger."

"And you just stared?  Fool! Gabelle, if this stranger comes into the village, lock him up." And he gave the order: "Drive on."

The château of Monsieur the Marquis was a big building.  A supper table was laid for two in one of the rooms.

"My nephew, Charles, has arrived?" asked the marquis.

"No," answered the head manservant.  "We

expected that he would arrive with Monsieur the Marquis."

"Well, leave the table as it is," said the marquis. "I'll be ready in a quarter of an hour."

He was half-way through his supper when the sound of wheels was heard.

"Ask my nephew to come straight to supper," said the marquis.

In a few minutes he came. He had been known in England as Charles Darnay.

The marquis received him very politely, but they did not shake hands.

"You have been a long time coming," said the marquis.

"No," said his nephew, "I have come straight here."

"Forgive me! I did not mean a long time on the journey. I meant a long time planning to make the journey."

"I was kept from making it by – a number of business matters."

"Of course," said his uncle.

They said nothing else until the servants had gone and uncle and nephew were alone together. Then:

"I have come back, uncle, to talk about the matter that took me away. It took me into great danger, but I expect you know about that. You may even have given some help to my enemies who brought me to trial in England."

At this, the marquis made a sign of polite

disagreement, but the cruel face showed clearly that it was only politeness.

"I believe I am lucky," said the nephew, "that you were received as coldly as ever by the great lords the day before yesterday. If you were not out of favour with the king and the great lords, I suppose a *lettre de cachet* would have sent me to one of the prisons to disappear – to be no trouble to you for an unknown length of time."

"You are tired," said the marquis. "Shall we end our talk for tonight?"

"One moment more. Sir, we have done wrong, and we shall pay for our great wrong-doing——"

"*We* have done wrong?" said the marquis, pointing first to his nephew and then to himself.

"Our family. We have done wrong to every man, woman and child who came between us and our pleasure. On her death-bed my mother – your sister – prayed that I would put right the many wrongs. And I have tried hard to get help to do so."

"You won't get help from me," said his uncle. "Good night."

Charles was led to a bedroom, and the marquis went to his own very fine and richly comfortable bedroom.

A few hours later, the great bell of the château was heard for a great distance over the fields and forest round the château, and even in the village, where the day's work had begun.

The servants had found Monsieur the Marquis. He was dead. Driven into his heart there was a knife. A piece of paper round it had the badly written words:

*Drive on. Drive him fast – to his death. This is from* GASPARD.

The tall man from Saint Antoine had made the marquis pay – pay more than a gold coin – for the death of his child.

# Chapter 5
## Two promises

A year passed.

Mr Charles Darnay had found work in England as a higher teacher of the French language. He also became known as a very good translator. He spent a part of each year at Cambridge University, and the rest of his time in London.

And he was in love.

On a summer day he went to a certain house in a quiet street in Soho. Dr Manette was reading a book. He was strong now in body and mind. He was always very glad to see Charles Darnay.

"Bring a chair here," he said, "and talk to me. Lucie is out at the moment, but she will soon be home."

"Dr Manette, I knew she was out. I wanted to speak to you."

There was silence for a moment. Then: "About Lucie?" asked the doctor.

"Yes," said Darnay. "I know that the love between you and your daughter is very great. And you certainly know that I am deeply in love with her."

"Have you any reason to believe that Lucie loves you?"

"No reason."

"So what do you want to ask me?" said the doctor.

"Only this: if Miss Manette ever speaks to you about me, will you not speak against me? If you can promise that, then there is something I must tell you. My present name, although it is not greatly changed from my mother's, is not my own. I want to tell you what my real name is, and why I am in England."

"Stop!" said Dr Manette.

"I want to have no secrets from you."

"Stop!" For a moment the doctor even had his hands over his ears. "Tell me when I ask you, not now. If Lucie loves you, you shall tell me on your marriage morning. Do you promise?"

"Certainly."

"Give me your hand. She will be home soon, and it is better that she should not see us together tonight. Go, and God bless you!"

When Lucie came home, she hurried upstairs. She was surprised to find her father's reading chair empty. She heard a low sound from his bedroom – the sound of making shoes.

"What shall I do?" she cried. But she hurried to his door and called softly to him. The shoemaking stopped at the sound of her voice, and he came out to her after a minute. They walked up and down together for a long time.

*Sydney Carton walks to Dr Manette's house*

She came down to look at him in his sleep that night. He was sleeping peacefully, and his shoemaking things were all as usual.

If Sydney Carton ever shone anywhere, he certainly never shone in Dr Manette's house. He visited it often, but he was usually silent and seemingly uninterested. When he felt like talking, he talked well, but it was not often. The cloud of carelessness nearly always hid any light that might have been inside him.

On a day in August, he went to the quiet street in Soho. Lucie was at her work, and he sat down near her table. She looked at his face, and there seemed to be a change in it.

"I'm afraid you aren't well, Mr Carton," she said.

"My way of living doesn't make one healthy, Miss Manette."

"That's very sad." She looked at him gently, and he was surprised to see tears in her eyes. "Can't you change your life?"

"It's too late for that," he said. "I'll never be a better man." All his usual carelessness seemed to have left him. "Please forgive me, Miss Manette," he said. "My sadness comes from what I want to say to you. Will you hear me?"

"If it will help you, Mr Carton, I'll be glad to listen."

"God bless you for your sweet pity. I want

you to know that you have been the last dream of my life. The sight of you with your father in this lovely home has made me remember the days when I had hope – the days before I began to waste my life."

"Can't I still do something to help you?" Lucie asked.

"Only this. Let me remember that I opened my heart to you, and that there was still something in me that you could pity. I know there is a great space between us. I know you can have no feeling besides pity for a man like me. But I want to promise that for you, and for anyone you love, I would do anything. I would give my life to keep a life you love beside you."

He said, "Goodbye!" and "God bless you!" and left her.

# Chapter 6
## Knitting

Madame Defarge was in her place in the wine-shop in Saint Antoine. Her husband was not in the shop, but more customers than usual seemed to be waiting for something.

After a time, Defarge arrived, dusty and tired. With him, also dusty and tired from a long walk, was an old road-mender with a blue cap. Madame Defarge gave the old man wine and bread, while three customers went, one at a time, to the room at the top of the stairs. Then Defarge took the road-mender upstairs to the room.

"This," said Defarge to the three men, "is the witness I told you about. Speak, Jacques. Tell them what you told me."

"I first saw your friend Gaspard one year ago. He was under the carriage of the marquis who is dead." And the road-mender told them about the death of the marquis. "After that, we hid him. And then your people hid him. But after a year, the government spies found him at last. The soldiers took him and hanged him in the village square, twelve metres high. They said it was for a lesson to the village people."

"Good," said one of the men. "You have told us what we wanted to know. Please wait for a few minutes outside the door."

Then Defarge and the three Saint Antoine men talked about the road-mender's story and the death of Gaspard.

"Then we all agree," said Defarge in the end. "The St Evrémonde family must be registered for destruction."

"Yes," they said. "The château and all the family, to be destroyed completely."

"Defarge," one of them said, "is it certain that there can be no problems about our way of keeping the register?"

"My friend," answered Defarge, "if my wife kept the register just by remembering it, there would be no mistakes. But with the register in her knitting, not one name, not one fact can be lost."

Later that evening, Defarge told his wife, "We were stopped at the gate as usual. Our friend in the police told me that another spy has been sent to Saint Antoine. He is an Englishman."

"His name?"

"Barsad."

"First name?"

"John."

"John Barsad," Madame Defarge said. "Do we know what he looks like?"

"Age, about forty; height, one metre seventy-seven; black hair; rather good-looking; face, thin, long and unhealthy; nose, not straight but turning towards the left."

Madame Defarge laughed. "That's good," she said. "I'll add him to the register tomor-row."

The next day, Madame Defarge was in her usual place when a newcomer entered the wine-shop. Madame Defarge did not look at him, but she picked up a rose from the table and put it in her hair.

It was surprising: the moment Madame Defarge picked up the rose, the customers stopped talking. One after another, they remembered something that made them leave the wine-shop.

"Good morning, madame," said the newcomer.

"Good morning, sir," she said. But to herself she added: "Ha! Good morning, age about forty, height one metre seventy-seven, black hair, rather good-looking, face thin, long and unhealthy, nose not straight but turning to the left. Yes, good morning." And she started her knitting again. "JOHN," she said to herself. "Stay long enough, and I'll knit 'BARSAD' before you go."

"I've heard a lot about you," the spy said to Defarge when the wine-shop keeper came in.

"Have you?"

"Yes. When Dr Manette was let out of that fearful prison, the Bastille, you took charge of him."

Madame Defarge's sign to her husband

meant: "Answer. But make your answers short."

"Yes," said Defarge.

"It was to you that his daughter came, with a man from a bank, to take him to England."

"Yes," said Defarge.

"Very interesting!" said the spy. "I have met Dr Manette and his daughter in England."

"Oh?"

"Yes. Miss Manette is going to be married. Not to an Englishman, but to a Frenchman. It is interesting that she is going to marry the nephew of the marquis for whose death your friend Gaspard was hanged so high. In other words, she is going to marry the present Marquis St Evrémonde. But he lives in England, unknown. He is not a marquis there. He is Mr Charles Darnay – d'Aulnais is the name of his mother's family."

Madame Defarge knitted without seeming to be interested in the spy's words. But the spy was a good enough spy to see that Defarge was troubled by the information.

After the spy had gone, Defarge said to his wife, "Can it be true?"

"As he has said it, it is probably a lie. But it may be true."

## Chapter 7
## A marriage

The marriage day was sunny and bright.

Lucie and Mr Lorry were ready to go to the church. They were waiting outside the door of the doctor's room, where he and Charles Darnay were talking.

The door of the doctor's room opened, and he came out with Charles Darnay. Dr Manette's face was white – which it had not been when they went in together. But he showed no anxiety as he took his daughter to the waiting carriage.

From the church where Charles Darnay and Lucie were married, they returned to the house in the quiet street. There was a happy meal, and then the newly married Mr and Mrs Darnay left for a short holiday.

It was when the doctor and Mr Lorry were alone in the hall that Mr Lorry saw a great change in the doctor.

For nine days, the doctor made shoes. There was the same lost look in his eyes that Mr Lorry remembered from the time in Saint Antoine. Mr Lorry was very anxious. In a letter to Lucie he had said nothing about the shoemaking, but Charles and Lucie were to come back from their holiday on the tenth day. Mr Lorry did everything he could think of

*Charles and Lucie leave the church after their marriage*

to help his friend.   He even spent his nights in Soho.   It was on the ninth night of anxious watching that sleep won the battle.   On the tenth morning Mr Lorry was woken by the sun shining in through the window.   He hurried to the door of the doctor's room.   The shoemaking things had been put on one side again, and the doctor was sitting, reading, at the window.   His face was still white, but he was quietly reading his book, and quietly interested in it.

Charles and Lucie made their home in the rooms above the part of the house Dr Manette lived in.

One of the first people to visit them to wish them well was Sydney Carton.   When he had gone, Lucie spoke to her husband about him.

"I'm afraid there is nothing we can do to make him change his way of life.   We can hardly hope for such a change.   But I want you to believe that he has a heart that is almost always hidden.   There are deep wounds in that heart, I am sure.   I am certain that he *can* do good things, gentle things, even noble things."

"I'll always remember it," Charles said.

Time passed, and Lucie held another life in her arms, another Lucie.

More time passed.   It was about little Lucie's sixth birthday that news began to come from France of a great storm rising in that country.

One night in July 1789, Mr Lorry came late to Soho from Tellson's.

"We have had so much business all day that we haven't known which way to turn. There is so much anxiety in Paris that our customers there can't give us the care of their money fast enough. They all want to send it to England."

"It's a bad sign," said Darnay.

"I agree," said Mr Lorry, "but I must be allowed to be angry about so much work. I'm not as young as I was. Is it too late for a cup of tea, Lucie?"

"Of course not. We kept the tea for you."

# Chapter 8
## The storm rises

A great roar came up from Saint Antoine. It was a storm of sound rising from a great crowd. The centre of the storm was Defarge's wine-shop, and Defarge himself was there. From him came the weapons – guns, axes, swords, knives, bars of iron and wood – that the people were waving.

"Come on, then!" cried Defarge. "We are ready now! To the Bastille!"

"Come on, women!" cried his wife. "We can kill as well as the men can, when the Bastille is taken."

They came on, wave after wave, against the great prison with its huge walls and eight great towers.

The attack went on for four hours. Defarge himself was at a big gun that he and his men had taken from the enemy.

At last a white flag appeared on one of the great towers. The governor wanted to talk.

The great stormy sea rose. With a roar, the people followed Defarge into the prison. They separated there, and went to look in every part of the building for:

"The prisoners! The prisoners of the aris-tocrats!"

Defarge took hold of one of the prison

*The crowd storms the Bastille*

officers. "Show me the North Tower!" he said. "Quick!"

"I will," said the frightened officer. "But there's nobody there."

In the North Tower, the prison officer showed Defarge and his friends the small, dark, stone-walled room that was "One hundred and five, North Tower".

Defarge found "A.M." cut in a stone in one wall.

"Alexandre Manette," he said. And he forced the stone out of the wall. Other stones were forced from their places, until at last Defarge found something that he was looking for. Then he was ready to go down and join the roaring crowd.

The storm continued in Paris, and it spread all over the country. Parties of wild-looking men moved north, south, east and west. They visited towns and villages, bringing hope to the miserable people, and danger to the nobles and their friends.

One party of such men came to the road-mender's village. After their visit, the château burnt.

There was great joy in the village as the fire in the château lit the village square. The people danced there in the square. Then one of them remembered that a part of Gabelle's work was gathering taxes, and the people ran to his house. Gabelle locked his doors and windows and put bars on them. He climbed on to his roof and hid there. The people danced and sang and shouted in front of his house until daylight, and then they went home, and Gabelle was safe for a time. He had no real enemies in the village.

The storm continued in France. The nobles left the country in large numbers. Those who escaped to England often went to Tellson's Bank in London for business and for news of their friends.

It was soon after little Lucie's ninth birthday that Charles Darnay went to the bank to speak to Mr Lorry.

"You are telling me," said the banker, "that at nearly eighty years of age I ought not to be going to Paris tonight?"

"Unsettled weather, a long journey, uncertain travelling, a country without order, a city that may not be safe, even for you——"

"My dear Charles, those are some of the reasons for my going, not for staying here. Somebody who knows Tellson's business well has to go. Most of my work there will be to pick out the papers and books that must be destroyed or hidden because they might put lives in danger."

"I wish I were going," said Darnay, more to himself than to Mr Lorry. "I can't stop thinking that a man like me might help to end the killing and destruction. I have been sorry for the people, and I have given them what I could. So they might listen to me. Only last night, I was saying to Lucie——"

"Lucie!" Mr Lorry said. "You stand there and talk about going to France. And in the same breath you speak the name of your lovely wife——"

Darnay smiled. "But I'm not going to France. You are, and it makes me anxious about you."

At that moment the office chief put an un-opened letter on Mr Lorry's desk. It was very dirty, but Darnay could read the address on it: "URGENT. To Monsieur the Marquis St Evré-monde in the care of Tellson's Bank, London, England."

This was Charles Darnay's own name. Only he and Dr Manette knew it. He had told the doctor his family name on his marriage morn-ing, and the doctor had made him promise to keep it a secret. Even Lucie and Mr Lorry did not know it.

"We still haven't found this marquis," said the office chief.

"I know where to find him," said Darnay. "Shall I take the letter?"

"Please do," said Mr Lorry.

Darnay took it out, and found a quiet place to read it.

Prison of the Abbaye, Paris
21 June 1792

Monsieur the Marquis.

I am in prison and in danger of my life. Only you can save me.

The reason I am here, they say, is that I acted against the people for an emigrant. I have shown them that I acted *for* the people, not against them; that, following your orders, I took no taxes, and I used all the money from your lands to help the people. Their only answer is that I have acted for an emigrant, and they ask where that emigrant is.

Oh, Monsieur the Marquis, if this letter reaches you, will you come and save me? I am here because I obeyed you, and that has put me in great danger.

Your obedient servant,
*Gabelle*

It was true that Darnay had given Gabelle written orders to let the people have everything possible. He himself had taken nothing; he had earned his own living in England.

That night, he wrote two letters. One was to Lucie; it gave her the reasons why he must go to Paris; and it showed her that there would be no danger to him there. The other was to Dr Manette, asking him to look after Lucie and their dear child; this letter, too, made it clear that, as a friend of the people, he would be quite safe in France.

Travelling in France in 1792 was very hard. Besides the bad roads, bad carriages, and bad horses, there were a lot of difficulties. Every town gate and village entrance had its group of citizens on guard. They stopped all travellers, questioned them, looked at their papers. Then they turned them back, or sent them on, or held them – just as they thought best for the new Republic of Liberty, Equality and Fraternity.

Charles Darnay had to show, again and again, the letter from the unhappy Gabelle in the prison of the Abbaye. In the end, at one small town on the road, he was given three citizens to guard him. He had to pay for this guard – which was more like a prisoner's guard.

At last they reached the entrance to Paris. There the guard at the gate – some soldiers, and many more citizens with guns – called out a strong-looking chief.

"Where are the papers of this prisoner?" he asked.

Charles Darnay did not like that. He said, "I am not a prisoner. I am a free traveller, and I have paid for this guard."

"Where," the same man asked again, "are the papers of this prisoner?"

One of Darnay's guards had them, and passed them to the chief. When he read

Gabelle's letter, the chief seemed surprised. He looked closely at Darnay.

"Follow me," he said. And he led Darnay to the guard-room.

An officer there looked at a register and picked up a pen.

"Citizen Defarge," he said to the strong-looking chief, "is this the emigrant Evrémonde?"

"This is the man."

"I am sending you, Evrémonde, to the prison of La Force."

"Why?" asked Darnay. "I have come here freely in answer to that letter in front of you. I want to speak for him. Isn't that my right?"

"Emigrants have no rights. It is the new law." The officer wrote a note, and gave it to Defarge, saying: "Guard him well."

# Chapter 9
# The Bastille prisoner

Mr Jarvis Lorry was living in the building that Tellson's Bank used in Paris. The bank was well guarded, but he knew that he could serve it best by living there. From the streets beyond the high wall and the strong gate, fearful sounds came today.

"Thank God," he thought, "that no one near and dear to me is in this fearful city tonight."

His door suddenly opened, and two people ran in: Lucie and her father!

"What has happened?" cried Mr Lorry, jumping up. "What has brought you here?"

"Charles!" Lucie said. "He's in Paris! He came here to help an old family servant. He was stopped at the gate, and they sent him to prison."

There were shouts outside, and the doctor went to the window.

"Don't look out!" Mr Lorry said. "It isn't safe."

"My dear friend," said the doctor, "nobody is as safe in Paris – in France – as I am. I was a Bastille prisoner, and my suffering at that time has given me a power now – a power that has brought us safely to Paris through all the guard points, and has given us news of Charles."

"What prison is he in?" asked Mr Lorry.

"La Force."

"Lucie, my dear," said the banker, "you must be very brave and do just what I say. You must let me put you in my room at the back while I talk to your father for two minutes."

Lucie obeyed, and Mr Lorry hurried back to Dr Manette.

"The crowd are murdering the prisoners, Manette. They come here to sharpen their weapons." He partly opened the window, and Dr Manette saw a crowd of men, their faces and clothes red with blood. "If, Doctor Manette, you really have the power you say – and I believe you have – make yourself known to these men. Get them to take you to La Force. It may be too late, but there is a chance you can save him."

Dr Manette shook his old friend's hand and hurried out. Mr Lorry, back at the window, saw him pushing his way to the middle of the crowd, turning their weapons away with his hand. For a few moments, he seemed to be talking to the leaders. Then a line of men hurried out, with the doctor in the middle of the line. They were shouting: "Make way for the Bastille prisoner! Save the Bastille prisoner's friend in La Force!"

Mr Lorry and Lucie had a long anxious wait. At last Dr Manette sent a short note: "Charles is safe, but I cannot come away yet."

Lucie did not know until long afterwards that on that day and during the next three days the angry people killed more than a thousand prisoners.

Dr Manette was taken to meet a group of men who had made themselves judges in La Force. The prisoners were brought to these self-made judges one at a time, and they were sent to their deaths or set free. Darnay had not yet appeared in front of these judges. They showed great joy at meeting the doctor, a man who had been a prisoner in the Bastille, without a reason and without any trial, for eighteen years. Charles Darnay was sent for, and Dr Manette spoke for him.

It seemed that the judges were just going to set the prisoner free. But something happened to make the judges talk secretly among themselves. The result was that Charles was sent back into the prison. But they promised that he would be safe until his trial in a real court.

Charles Darnay remained in prison for a year. The doctor could do nothing to get him out or to arrange an earlier trial.

At last the news came that Darnay was being sent to the prison of the Conciergerie. His trial was to be the next day. Lucie hurried to tell Mr Lorry the news. He took her in his arms and dried her eyes.

"Don't cry, my dear. Your father will speak

for him, and everybody in Paris is on Dr Manette's side."

There was somebody in the next room. Lucie did not know who it was. Sydney Carton had just arrived from England. He did not want Lucie to know that he was in Paris, but Mr Lorry repeated her news clearly so that the unknown visitor would hear: "Taken to the Conciergerie. For trial tomorrow."

The fearful court sat every day, with the same five judges, the same lawyer for the Republic, and the same jury of "good citizens" who would say whether the people on trial – men or women or children – should live or go to the guillotine.

Charles Darnay's trial began just like hundreds of other trials in that court, and the crowd in the great hall showed little interest at first.

The lawyer for the Republic spoke first. Charles Evrémonde, called Darnay, was denounced as an emigrant. The law was that an emigrant who came back to France must be put to death – must go to the guillotine. It was a new law, made since Darnay had come back, but it was the law.

"Take off his head!" shouted the people in the court. "An enemy of the Republic! An aristocrat! To the guillotine!"

But the judge wanted to hear Darnay's

witnesses: Gabelle and Alexandre Manette. The good doctor's name brought cheers and excited shouts from the crowd. Through these witnesses, Charles was able to show: that he had not become the marquis when his uncle was killed; that he had gone to another country to work for his living; that he had not lived on the work of the people; that he had given to the people all that he could.

The shouts in the court changed:

"That's enough! Let him go! Set the good doctor's friend free! And set Gabelle free! Evrémonde is the people's friend!"

The judge was just going to let Darnay go as "Not guilty" when, once more, something happened to make a change.

The lawyer for the Republic said that he must call witnesses *against* the prisoner. There were shouts of anger, but the judge asked, "Who are these witnesses?"

"Ernest Defarge, wine-seller of Saint Antoine."

"Good," said the judge.

"Alexandre Manette, doctor."

There was a roar in the court. Doctor Manette stood up. "Who dares to say that I have anything against the husband of my dear child?"

"Dear child?" said the judge. "Nothing can be dearer to a good citizen than the Republic. You must sit down and be silent."

Defarge told the court how, as a boy, he worked for the doctor. He had taken the doctor secretly into his house when the governor of the Bastille let him out of prison. And he spoke about the state the doctor was in, and the shoemaking.

"I knew," he said, "that the doctor was in 'One hundred and five, North Tower'. When the Bastille was taken ('Thanks to fearless citizens like you!' shouted a voice) I went to the North Tower. There, hidden behind a stone, I found the paper that you, the judge, have in your hands. The writing is the writing of Alexandre Manette."

"Read the paper," the judge ordered.

In December 1757, Dr Manette's hidden paper said, the doctor was walking beside the river in Paris when a carriage stopped near him. Two men with swords made him get into the carriage. They took him to a house outside Paris, to the bedside of a dying woman. She was out of her mind, and there was very little that the doctor could do for her.

In another room in the house, a boy was dying. He was dying of a sword wound. He was the woman's brother, and it was he who told Dr Manette the story.

The woman and her brother were poor workers on the land of the Marquis St Evrémonde. The marquis saw the woman. She was beautiful, and he desired her. Aristocrats in France at that time thought they could take any woman from among the workers on their land, and the Marquis St Evrémonde took the boy's sister after killing her husband. The boy went to save her, and the marquis wounded him with his sword.

The doctor tried hard to save the lives of both the boy and his sister. It was impossible. The boy died first. His sister lived for another week, with Dr Manette at her bedside, before she died.

The marquis tried to give the doctor money, but he would not take it. He wondered what he ought to do. In the end, he wrote privately to the government minister, asking him what he should do.

A few evenings later, a message came to the doctor's house. The message was that he was needed urgently at a house in the next street. He hurried out. Hands took hold of him from behind. Cloths were tied round his mouth and his arms. The marquis came towards him. "Yes, that's the man," he said. Then he took from his pocket the letter that Dr Manette had written to the minister. "You fool!" he said. "Did you expect this to reach the minister? Look." He showed the letter to the doctor. and then he set fire to it at a lamp that one of his men carried. "Take him away!"

The Marquis's servants hurried Dr Manette

*Defarge tells the court about Dr Manette*

away.   They took him to the Bastille.

The paper was written after the doctor's first ten years in the prison.   It ended:

> "If God had put it into the hard heart of the Marquis St Evrémonde to let me have news of my dear wife, I might have forgiven him. But I have heard nothing.   Nothing! Now I, Alexandre Manette, unhappy prisoner, denounce him.   I denounce him and every person in his guilty family.   In the day when these things will be judged, I call for punishment for them, and for their children and their children's children, to the last one."

A great roar went up.   The doctor's story was of the kind that caused the greatest anger against all aristocrats at that time.   There was nothing that the court could say except: "Guilty.   At heart, and by his family blood, an aristocrat, Evrémonde is an enemy of the Republic.   Back to the Conciergerie, and death at the guillotine tomorrow."

## Chapter 10
## A promise kept

The spy, Barsad, was now working at the Conciergerie. He guarded the prisoners. As he came out of the Conciergerie, he was stopped by an Englishman. The man was so like Darnay, who had just been taken into the prison, that the spy was surprised and rather frightened.

"You needn't be afraid," said Sydney Carton. "You are in no danger *if* you help me."

"Why should I help you?"

"Well, a spy paid by the republican French government was, not long ago, a spy paid by the aristocratic English government! If you are denounced, they will think you are still working secretly against the Republic for the English aristocrats and their friends, the emigrant French aristocrats."

Barsad looked frightened. It was true. He would be in danger.

"So what do you want?" he asked.

"Not very much. You work in the Conciergerie?"

"Escape from the Conciergerie is not possible," the spy said.

"Who said anything about an escape?"

Sydney Carton went to see his old friend Mr Lorry at Tellson's Paris office. Dr Manette was there, white, ill, not knowing what had happened or where he was.

"You are leaving Paris very soon, aren't you, Lorry?" said Carton. "Can you leave tomorrow, and take Lucie and Manette, to save them? There is nothing you or they can do now. And there is danger for them if they stay. You have your paper letting you leave the city and the country?"

"Yes."

"Let's look at Dr Manette's papers."

They looked in the doctor's coat pockets. There were papers there for himself and Lucie.

"Good," said Carton. "Now, Lorry, old friend, I want you to take my own papers for me. Look: 'Sydney Carton. Lawyer. English. To be allowed to pass all gates and guard posts.' Please look after that. I have something I must do, and I don't want to have that paper with me. Please listen very carefully. Have a carriage and horses here, ready to start, at two o'clock tomorrow afternoon – here! You must put Lucie and her father in it. Tell her that it is to save her father. Be in the carriage yourself at two o'clock. Wait until my seat is filled. Until my seat is filled! Then, for England as fast as the carriage can go!"

In the black prison of the Conciergerie, fifty-two people were waiting. They were to go to the guillotine that afternoon.

Charles Darnay knew that there was no hope now. He wrote a long letter to Lucie. It told her of his love. And it told her that he had known nothing of his family's part in her father's being sent to the Bastille and kept there.

One o'clock struck.

Footsteps in the passage. The key turned in the door.

Someone came in. Charles Darnay could hardly believe his eyes. Standing there, smiling, but with a warning finger to his lips, stood Sydney Carton.

"I have come from her, Darney. You must do what she wants you to do. Change clothes with me quickly."

"There is no escape from here, Sydney. You'll only die with me if you try anything."

"Who said anything about an escape? You must do what she wants... Now take that pen and write."

"What shall I write? – Is that a weapon in your hand? No. It looks more like a bottle. – Who must I write to?"

"Nobody. Just write what I say. Write: 'You remember the promise I made. I am glad the time has come to show that——'"

Charles Darnay was writing "to show that", when the opened bottle came under his nose, and he knew no more.

Sydney Carton moved quickly. He made Darnay's hair and clothes look careless like his own. He tied his own hair carefully, like Darnay's. Then he went to the door and called Barsad.

"Look," he said. "There is no danger to you, Barsad, if you do what you promised. Take him out. Saying goodbye to his old friend Darnay has made him faint, so you will need help. Take him to the carriage in the place I told you about. Put him in the carriage yourself. Show him to Mr Lorry. Tell Lorry to remember my words and drive away!"

Fifty-two people went to the guillotine that afternoon. One of them was a little sewing-woman. When the fifty-two were gathered together, she saw Sydney Carton and went to him.

"Citizen Evrémonde," she said. "I was with you in La Force. Do you remember me?"

"Yes," he said, "but I forget what you are here for."

"Somebody denounced me as an enemy of the Republic, although I have done nothing. I am not afraid, but I am little and weak. It will help me if I can hold your hand on the way to the guillotine."

As the anxious eyes were lifted to his face, he saw a sudden uncertainty in them, and then great surprise. He took the poor, work-worn fingers, and with the other hand he touched his lips.

"Are you dying for him?" she asked very quietly.

"And his wife and child. Yes. Hush!"

"Oh, will you let me hold your brave hand, stranger?"

"Hush! Yes, my poor sister. To the end of our journey."

A carriage drives up to the city gate.

"Papers!"

Jarvis Lorry has them all.

"Alexandre Manette. Doctor. French. Which is he? Ah! The poor old man is too old for the excitement of Paris in these days! It has made him ill. – Lucie, his daughter, the wife of Evrémonde. Her husband has displeased the Republic. That is easy in these days. – Sydney Carton. Lawyer. English. Which is he? Ah! He has fainted."

"Yes," Mr Lorry says. "But we believe the country air outside Paris will make him better."

"Jarvis Lorry. Banker. English. You? Yes. Here are the papers, then. Drive on! A good journey!"

There is the usual crowd at the guillotine. They are waiting for the tumbrils, the slow-moving farm carts that will bring the day's prisoners to the fearful engine of death. In front of the crowd there is a line of chairs. They are for the women who sit there and knit.

The tumbrils arrive. The people in the crowd push forward to see Charles Darnay, once the Marquis St Evrémonde. He is there, holding the hand of a little woman who does not look at all like an aristocrat. The knitting women see him and continue their knitting. One more aristocrat is to die.

It was said that the bravest of the fifty-two who went to the guillotine that day was the man they called Charles Evrémonde.

Perhaps, as Sydney Carton went to the guillotine in place of his friend, he saw something of the years that were to come. Perhaps his thoughts were:

"I see Lucie and Charles, the man for whom I am giving my life. They are living peaceful, useful and happy lives in England in a better future. Lucie has a son, and they call him Sydney Carton. Lucie's father gets back his health and strength. He is an old man, but he does good work among those who need a doctor's help. I see their old friend Mr Lorry visiting them more and more often for ten years before his quiet death.

"I see the young Sydney Carton Darnay becoming a great lawyer, and later a fine judge. One day he comes with his son to

*Sydney Carton goes to the guillotine*

this place – a place then of beauty, with none of today's ugliness. And he tells his son my story. His son also has the name Sydney Carton Darnay. He has a forehead that I know, and it is roughened in a way that I know as he listens quietly.

"It is a far, far better thing that I do than I have ever done. It is a far, far better rest that I go to than I have ever known."

# Questions

## Questions on each chapter

1 *From London to Dover*
  1 Where was Mr Lorry at the beginning of the story?
  2 Where did he go into a hotel?
  3 Who came to meet him at the hotel?
  4 What are the "customers" of a bank?
  5 Where were Mr Lorry and Miss Manette going?

2 *In Paris*
  1 What was the name of the wine-shop keeper?
  2 Where was the room he took them to?
  3 What was the man in the room doing?
  4 Who was the man in the room?
  5 What did Madame Defarge bring to the carriage?

3 *The trial*
  1 What was the prisoner's name?
  2 Who was the chief witness against the prisoner?
  3 What had the witness been in prison for?
  4 Who was Stryver?
  5 Who helped Stryver with his work?

4 *The marquis*
  1 Whose child did the marquis's carriage kill?
  2 Who probably threw the coin into the carriage?
  3 Who was the marquis's nephew?
  4 Why was the marquis unable to get a *lettre de cachet*?
  5 What happened to the marquis in the end?

5 *Two promises*
  1 Who was Darnay in love with?
  2 Why did the doctor ask Darnay to "Stop"?
  3 What did the doctor do after Darnay had gone?

4  Who had been the last dream of Sydney Carton's life?
5  What was Sydney Carton's promise?

## 6 Knitting
1  What happened to Gaspard in the end?
2  How did Madame Defarge keep the register?
3  What was the new spy's name?
4  How did Madame Defarge warn the customers in the wine-shop?
5  What information troubled Defarge?

## 7 A marriage
1  For how long did Charles and Lucie's holiday last?
2  What did the doctor do for nine of those days?
3  Where did Charles and Lucie make their home?
4  Who was "little Lucie"?

## 8 The storm rises
1  Where did the people of Saint Antoine get their weapons?
2  What great building did the people attack?
3  Where did Defarge go inside the prison?
4  Who was the letter addressed to?
5  Who had written the letter?
6  Where did the officer send Darnay?

## 9 The Bastille prisoner
1  What power did the doctor have in France?
2  What were the men doing outside the bank?
3  Why did Mr Lorry repeat Lucie's news clearly?
4  Who were the witnesses for Darnay?
5  Who were the witnesses against him?
6  Where had Defarge found Manette's paper?

## 10 A promise kept
1  Where was Barsad when Carton spoke to him?
2  What did Carton give to Mr Lorry?
3  How many prisoners were to go to the guillotine that day?
4  Which man went to the guillotine: Charles Darnay or Sydney Carton?
5  Which promise did he keep?

# Questions on the whole story

These are harder questions. Read the Introduction, and think hard about the questions before you answer them. Some of them ask for your opinion, and there is no fixed answer.

1 Doctor Manette:
   a Where was he in prison?
   b How long did he spend in prison?
   c Who caused him to be put in prison?
   d What happened to his wife?

2 Defarge:
   a Why was Dr Manette in Defarge's house when he came out of prison?
   b What did Defarge do just before the attack on the Bastille?
   c What did he do during the attack on the Bastille?
   d Why do you think he wanted to find "One hundred and five, North Tower"?

3 Mr Lorry:
   a He says, "I really am just a man of business without feelings."
      1 Who does he say it to, and when?
      2 Why does he say it?
      3 Do you think it is true? Can you give a reason for your answer?
   b What very difficult question do you think he asked himself when Barsad brought Charles Darnay to the carriage?
   c What answer did he give himself?
   d Why, in your opinion, did he give that answer?

4 Sydney Carton:
   a In what ways do you think his character was bad?
   b How did he show the good part of his character?
   c What did the little sewing-woman know about him?
   d Do you, yourself, find him likeable? Can you give a reason for your answer?

5 Which of the people in the story do you like best? Why?

6 Do you like the ending of this story, with Sydney Carton giving his life for Charles Darnay? Can you give a reason for your answer?

# New words

anxiety
    a feeling of fear that
    something bad may
    happen; **anxious** = having
    a feeling of anxiety

customer
    someone who buys things
    from a shop; someone who
    uses a bank

denounce
    name (someone) openly as
    a wrongdoer or an enemy

destroy
    put an end to; pull to
    pieces; **destruction** =
    breaking completely

emigrant
    someone who has left their
    own country to go and live
    in another country

faint
    lose thought and feeling
    (and fall down)

forehead
    the part of the face above
    the eyes and eyebrows

guilty
    having broken a law

knit
    use two or more long pins
    (**knitting needles**) to make a
    kind of loose cloth
    (**knitting**) out of wool

noble
    of very fine character; (a
    man) of one of the ruling
    families (the **aristocrats**)

register
    a list (for example, of
    people who must be
    punished); add (a name) to
    a list

roar
    (make) a deep, very loud
    sound (like an angry crowd)

sign
    something (for example, a
    movement of the hand) that
    has a meaning

spy
    someone who watches
    secretly or gets secret
    information

trial
    a hearing (usually by a
    judge) of what is said for
    and against a prisoner

urgent
    very important, and
    needing to be dealt with at
    once

witness
    someone who has seen
    what happened (and is
    made to tell about it at a
    **trial**)